HIP HOP HUSTLE

BY JAKE MADDOX

Text by Dolores Andral
Illustrated by Mario Gushiken

STONE ARCH BOOKS
a capstone imprint

Published by Stone Arch Books, an imprint of Capstone
1710 Roe Crest Drive, North Mankato, Minnesota 56003
capstonepub.com

Library of Congress Cataloging-in-Publication Data
Names: Maddox, Jake, author. | Andral, Dolores, author. | Gushiken,
    Mário, illustrator.
Title: Hip-hop hustle / Jake Maddox ; text by Dolores Andral ; illustrated
    by Mario Gushiken.
Description: North Mankato, Minnesota : Stone Arch Books, an imprint of
    Capstone, [2024] | Series: Jake Maddox sports stories | Audience: Ages
    8 to 11. | Audience: Grades 4–6. | Summary: Chery Etienne has her own
    hip-hop dance crew, but now some of them are moving away and she
    will have to try out for her middle school's hip-hop dance team, although
    since she has never had any formal training she is not sure her unique
    style will be welcome.
Identifiers: LCCN 2022047876 (print) | LCCN 2022047877 (ebook) |
    ISBN 9781669033370 (hardcover) | ISBN 9781669033332 (paperback) |
    ISBN 9781669033349 (pdf) | ISBN 9781669033363 (epub)
Subjects: LCSH: Hip-hop dance—Juvenile fiction. | Dance teams—Juvenile
    fiction. | Dance—Competitions—Juvenile fiction. | Self-confidence—
    Juvenile fiction. | CYAC: Hip-hop dance—Fiction. | Dance teams—
    Fiction. | Contests—Fiction. | Self-confidence—Fiction.
Classification: LCC PZ7.M25643 Hi 2024 (print) | LCC PZ7.M25643 (ebook)
    | DDC 813.6 [Fic]--dc23/eng/20221227
LC record available at https://lccn.loc.gov/2022047876
LC ebook record available at https://lccn.loc.gov/2022047877

Designer: Sarah Bennett

TABLE OF CONTENTS

CHAPTER ONE

THE LAST DANCE

"Five-six-seven-eight!" Chery Etienne shouted and snapped her fingers to her favorite song. Chery and her dance squad—The Chery Bars—got into position. They bounced softly on their heels and casually looked around. But when the rap started, The Bars went hard. They danced at 100 percent—stomping, pumping their arms, twisting, and sliding.

Chery hopped in front. Her legs and hips moved one way while her arms and upper body moved another. The Bars followed.

Chery rolled her shoulders and dipped. She placed her hands on her knees one at a time to the beat.

"Yeah! Yeah!" Chery yelled over the music. "And jump!"

Chery tapped Jordyn in. Jordyn moved out front and led the dance. Then she nodded at Chery. They pretended to lasso the other members of the squad, Day-Day and Jolan. The boys leaned back like they were being pulled. When the beat dropped again, they all waved their arms, "breaking loose."

"And jump!" Chery called. Everyone landed with a hard stomp.

"Jolan, go!" Chery yelled.

"Oh!" Jolan said, shaking his hands to signal he forgot. "I'm used to Kioko going first."

"Kioko hasn't danced with us since June," Chery said, stopping the music.

Kioko Tabata used to be a part of the squad. Now Chery's dance squad consisted of Daniel "Day-Day" Abelman, twins Jolan and Jordyn Jackson, and herself.

"Honestly, Kioko not being here throws me off too," Jordyn said, dropping to the ground. "I wish she didn't have to change schools." Sweat covered Jordyn's face.

They were all sweaty. Chery took a swig from her water bottle.

"I hope she makes it to the dance-a-thon next month," Chery said. "She's the only one who can do my signature move with me."

"The Chery on Top!" the others said.

Chery whipped her waist-length box braids around, brought one leg up straight, and spun. With her leg still in the air, she fell into a split. Then she slid up and fell back down into a split in the other direction.

Her squad clapped loudly.

"That's definitely a showstopper!" Day-Day said. "But Kioko plays rugby now at her new school." He draped a towel over his head.

"What if we didn't do the dance-a-thon?" Jordyn said, giving her brother a look.

"No dance-a-thon?" Chery asked. She jumped up and did a moonwalk side glide.

"Our dad said we have our entire lives to dance," Jolan added.

Chery stopped gliding and grabbed Jordyn's and Jolan's hands. "This is the last summer with our squad! You guys are moving to Germany, and Kioko already left because of private school. We have to make this year's dance-a-thon count!"

Chery cued the music on her phone. She snapped her fingers again.

"Come on," Cherry said, "we only have a few more weeks to perfect our dance. Five-six-seven-eight!"

Instead of moving left, like they practiced, Chery fell to her knees. She twirled and jumped back up again. She was just in time to move to the right with everyone else.

"What are you doing?" Jolan asked, mis-stepping. "You messed me up! Why'd you change the routine?"

"You know me!" Chery replied. "My body grooves how it wants!"

"You always do your own thing!" Jolan complained. "I'm tired of starting and stopping. I'm tired of practices. I'm tired of sweating. I quit!"

Chery knew Jolan picked fights when something was bothering him. And she thought about the look he'd shared with Jordyn earlier. And the fact that they both talked about not dancing anymore.

"Guys, what's going on?" Chery asked. "You both seem off today."

Jordyn took a deep breath. "We're moving to the military base at the beginning of August. Our dad thinks it's better to make friends over there before school starts."

Chery's face fell. "That's in three weeks," she said. "I thought I had one more dance left with my squad!"

"You and Daniel can perform as a duo," Jolan said.

"Actually, this kind of works out for me too," Day-Day said. "Between private ballroom dance lessons and dancing with our squad, I could use a break."

Chery felt her heart deflate.

"But I'm taking a break from ballroom dancing in the fall," Day-Day quickly added. "And I'm going to join the school's hip-hop dance team in September. You should too!"

Join the school team? That option was even worse.

Chery had her own squad—it even had her name. Besides, she had never joined a dance team because her mom said getting to the practices was too difficult.

But Chery knew that wasn't the only reason. She had once overheard her mom talking about it on the phone. Dance classes were also too expensive.

CHAPTER TWO

NO-CUT SPORT

Rap music blared from speakers in the auditorium. Chery felt it in her heart. But it wasn't why her heart was thumping fast. Today was the first day of school, and she was auditioning for the Ess Robinson Middle School hip-hop dance team. About twenty other students crowded onto the stage.

Chery stood in the second row behind Day-Day. He turned toward her, waving two big thumbs up.

Day-Day wasn't worried. He'd been taking dance lessons since he was five years old. But Chery didn't know the first thing about tryouts.

The dance coach, Miss Miller, joined them onstage. "I grew up dancing ballet," she said. "But I love the freeness of hip-hop. Unlike in ballet, your moves don't have to be exact. I want you to have the choices I wish I'd had as a young dancer. This is your dance team. I'm going to rely on you for ideas."

Miss Miller began the audition by teaching a dance combination. She put different moves together, counting each one until she reached eight. Chery and her squad kind of practiced that way. But instead of using numbers, they used words like *bomp, zoop, gah,* and *ayy!*

"Let's practice that combo two more times," Miss Miller yelled over the music. "But after the last eight-count, I want to see some improvisation. Show off your moves!"

Chery beamed. You didn't have a dance squad without having moves. After repeating the second combo, she quickly performed some of her favorite moves. Then she lifted her leg for the Chery on Top move—but Ana crashed into her.

"Sorry!" Chery said.

"We're supposed to be showcasing our talents," Ana Alvarez Aces said, narrowing her eyes. Aces wasn't Ana's real last name, but that's what everyone called her because she aced everything she did.

Chery tried to explain her signature move, but Ana scoffed. "This isn't amateur hour," she said.

Talking with Ana made Chery miss the next set of combinations. Miss Miller was already counting the next combo, and Chery quickly got lost. Instead of moving forward on the three-count, she moved sideways and landed on Ana's foot.

"Ow!" Ana said.

Chery crisscrossed instead of gliding, tripping up some of the other dancers. She completed a full turn instead of a half-turn. And as everyone moved left, Chery moved right. She even crashed into some of them.

Miss Miller must have been looking the other way. Because when the combination was over, she clapped.

"Well done!" she said, smiling. "You're all amazing dancers." Then she called Ana up to the front of the class.

Ana put all the combinations together with no mistakes, just like Miss Miller showed them. For the first time in her life, Chery wished she'd had actual dance lessons. Then maybe she wouldn't look and feel like such an amateur.

* * *

The next day, the audition results were in.
Two pieces of paper were taped to the doors of
the auditorium.

Chery waited for the hallway to clear
before she checked. She and Day-Day walked
together. Her heart pounded as she neared
the door.

"You got this," Day-Day said.

Chery peered up at the paper. She spotted
Day-Day's last name—Abelman—above
Alvarez. Then she spotted her own: Etienne.

"See! Told you!" Day-Day said.

Suddenly, Ana appeared behind them.

"Everyone made it," she said, rolling her
eyes. "It's a no-cut sport."

CHAPTER THREE

DANCE OFF

For the next two months, Chery and the rest of the dance team practiced three days a week. They needed a solid routine for the regional competition being held before winter break.

Then one afternoon, Miss Miller practically leaped onto the stage. "I have a really great opportunity for one of you," she said. "I just found out a slot has opened for a solo dancer in a touring dance competition."

A soft murmur filled the room.

"That means one of you lucky dancers can compete!" Miss Miller continued. "It's in a few weeks, but the registration fees are paid, and a spot is reserved."

The students erupted in applause.

Ana raised her hand. "You know how the boys football team is undefeated?" she said. "And the girls cross-country team is headed to the state tournament? I think the most seasoned dancer should represent the school." Ana flipped her hair. "So we can keep the school's winning streak going."

"I came in first place in the jazz finals over the summer," Trina Bell said.

"Pick me!" Kai Victor said. "I'm gonna be there with my brother anyway for his all-star dance team performance." He jumped out of his seat with his arms at ninety-degree angles. "See my robot!"

Miss Miller waved her hands in the air. "Every single one of you has talent. But this competition is about more than just winning. It's about preparation, showmanship, and *learning*."

"So, then who gets to go?" Ana asked.

"This is a team sport. I think it should be a team decision," Miss Miller said.

"How?" several voices asked.

"A dance battle!" Day-Day shouted, looking at Chery. Shouts of glee erupted.

Chery smiled. Dance battles were what her squad did for fun! But moments later, only seven students, including Chery and Ana, lined up for the challenge. Not even Day-Day stepped up.

"You got this," he whispered in Chery's ear.

"Let's start with our warm-up routine," Miss Miller said. The dancers started doing the familiar combo.

But not Chery. She waited for the music to speak to her. When the right sound hit, Chery's body popped. She raised her knee right when the music went high. And dropped it when it went low. Then she dropped to her knees and twirled up and repeated.

Oohs and aahs erupted around her.

"Everyone improvise," Miss Miller said after a while.

One by one, dancers ran out of moves, and bowed out. Soon, only Chery and Ana Aces were left. The students surrounded them.

"Since it's just the two of you," Miss Miller said, "let's put on new music."

As Chery waited for the right beat again, Ana moved first. She was confident and graceful. Her arms stretched long and wide. And when she bounced on her toes like a ballerina to the *thump-thump, bump-bump-bump,* she got big claps.

For her turn, Chery pumped her chest to start the challenge. She pointed two fingers from her eyes to Ana's, giving her a hard stare.

Chery shuffled her feet, heel to toe. Then, stepping close to Ana's face, Chery dropped her heel and slid backward.

The kids hooted and waved.

Ana came back with an arm wave to a body wave. Then she lifted one of her legs to her head and spun.

"Get it!" Kai shouted.

Chery rolled her head so her long braids whipped around and around. She lifted her leg, too, and ended with the Chery on Top move.

The class exploded in a huge round of applause.

"Cher-y! Cher-y! Cher-y!" some of the students shouted.

Miss Miller quieted the class. "Great dancing from all who participated. But it looks like you've decided—Chery is our winner!"

* * *

A week later, Chery and Day-Day were the first at dance practice when Fran Perkins hurried in and dropped her backpack. Several workbooks and a dance catalog spilled out. Chery helped Fran pick them up.

"Thanks," Fran said, placing the catalog on top of the pile. "By the way, do you know what you're wearing to the solo competition?"

More dancers filed into practice.

"Something funky, I hope," Kai said.

"It should be shiny," Nell Sunri said. "So you stand out."

"You have to go to DanceYes!" Fran said. "Ana's aunt owns it. Tell her you know Ana, and she'll hook you up."

"You *have* to look the part," Kai said, breaking into a robot dance and voice. "You must keep the streak! Keep the streak!"

As more dancers poured into practice, others joined him. "Keep the streak!" shouts grew.

Get a new outfit? Keep the streak? Chery just wanted to dance. But was everyone saying that without the right outfit, she wouldn't be good enough to keep the winning streak going?

CHAPTER FOUR

OLDIE BUT GOODIE

The next Saturday morning, Chery and her mom, Beatriz, set out to buy a dance outfit. Chery was tired and fell asleep almost instantly in the rocking car.

Before long, the lurching and jerking of her mom's parking woke Chery.

"This isn't the mall," Chery said, looking around.

"If you weren't asleep, you would have heard me say we're going to a pop-up flea market," Mom said, staring. "Did you stay up past your bedtime dancing again?"

"Only until midnight! I had to get my moves right," Chery said with a yawn.

"Sleep is just as important as practice, young lady," her mom replied.

"So is getting the right outfit," Chery said. "I need to go to DanceYes! Everyone said Ana's aunt has the best dance clothing."

"We can get something here," Mom said. "Remember your dance at the community center? When you and your squad wore those tracksuits? I found them in a place like this."

Chery remembered the suits. They were nice and stretchy. Perfect for doing splits.

* * *

Before long, Chery and her mom had been in and out of so many booths that Chery's feet were tired.

"These aren't even dance outfits," Chery said, flipping through old clothes hanging on a rack. "They're just regular clothes."

"Hip-hop fashion is about making what we wear our own," Mom said. "It's about whatever works for you and your squad."

"But I'm not with my squad anymore," Chery replied. "I'm on a school team now. And the other sports teams are on a winning streak. I don't want to be the one who jinxes it because I wore the wrong thing."

Beatriz hugged Chery. "You danced just as well in my oversized shirt, remember?"

Chery wondered if Mom was saying this to avoid buying her an expensive dance outfit.

Over a loudspeaker, a record scratched. It pounded with the base of a popular song. Across the way, in the center of the booths, two guys stared at each other. One had on a hoodie, the other wore skinny jeans. They walked toward each other like there was a problem. Their shoulders bumped. Just when it looked like trouble, the music switched, and they broke out into a dance.

Regular-looking people tossed their bags aside and stepped in line with the two dancers. It was a flash mob! It grew from two to five to twelve dancers. Men, women, boys, and girls in regular street clothes moved together.

Shoppers crowded around.

The music changed to an old rap song that talked about hip-hopping non-stopping. The dancers fanned out and formed two lines. Then, two-by-two, dancers battled. The two who shoulder-checked each other were the last to go. One moved like a puppet being pulled by strings. The crowd clapped in rhythm during his performance.

In a surprise move, his dance rival slid across the ground on his head. The shoppers howled. Then he swung his legs around in a windmill before freezing. That was definitely a showstopping move.

"He's good," Mom said.

When the dancer rose, his rival gave him a hug and a big pat on the back. They looked like they were having the best time.

After the performance ended, Mom leaned toward Chery. "Are you going to tell them *they* don't look like dancers?"

Chery couldn't imagine a group of better dancers.

She yanked her mom's arm. "You're right! We can get a perfect dance outfit here. Like that hat that girl was wearing. It would hold my braids!"

CHAPTER FIVE

SHOWTIME!

The following week, Chery practiced the moves Miss Miller helped polish for the solo competition. But like she did for most of her dances, Chery let the music speak to her, and she switched things up during the routine.

"You should stop changing it so close to the competition," Ana said. "You want muscle memory."

Chery tensed at Ana's words. Why was she suddenly giving her tips and advice?

"You've never been to a competition," Ana continued. "You want your moves to be automatic through repetition."

"That's true," Trina added. "Because when you're onstage, in front of the big lights, you'll be too nervous to think."

"One time my brother totally forgot his moves," Kai said. "It was embarrassing. But it happened because he didn't practice."

"This is why I love this class," Miss Miller said, stepping forward. "We can all learn from one another. I love Chery's self-expression and the moves she chose. She makes every dance her own. With plenty of practice, plus some of her own spontaneous moves, she'll do a great job onstage."

* * *

The night before the solo competition, Chery found it too hard to sleep. And by midnight, she was still awake.

She picked up her phone from her nightstand. Most nights Chery had to turn it in before bed. But Mom had allowed her to keep it for one night to set an alarm for the morning.

She hoped Day-Day had his phone too.

U up? can't sleep, she texted.

dance 2morrow! Day-Day texted back with a frowning emoji.

i know. help!!

put on fav show. u'll fall asleep super fast. i always do.

Chery found a dance competition online and settled in. She was sure she'd be asleep in no time.

Before long, one episode turned into six! Chery glanced over at her alarm clock. It read 3:07 a.m.! She couldn't believe how much time had passed. She needed to be up in three hours!

When the alarm blared, Chery felt like she had just closed her eyes. The clock had to be wrong. But soon, Mom was at her door singing, "Rise and dance!"

Twenty minutes later, Chery was in the car with her pillow. Her mom's voice cut in and out while Chery fell in and out of sleep.

The words "We're here!" finally woke Chery for good.

Mom opened her door and then paused. She touched Chery's head. "You feel okay?"

Chery couldn't admit to being up all night on her phone.

"Storing up my energy," she lied.

The hotel was sprawling. Dancers from kindergarten through high school moved in every direction. Many wore slippers and carried pillows. Others pulled rolling bags. Groups of dancers in leotards took selfies together. Bright lights shined everywhere.

Chery followed her mom like a duckling, looking for the correct sign-in table.

It took a long time to weave through the building and crowd. When they finally made it to the *Junior Solo, ages 9–11* table, the attendant found Chery's name.

"The dressing room is down the hall. Someone will come get you soon," the attendant said.

Chery didn't know there would be a room to change. She was already wearing her dance outfit—harem sweatpants, a graphic T-shirt, and an oversized hat.

The dressing room turned out to be a large conference room. Overnight bags and backpacks littered the floor. Groups of girls recorded themselves on their phones while dancing or talking or giggling. They changed into shimmery dresses, silk pants, or colorful costumes. Many wore makeup and had their straight hair pulled back into tight buns.

Chery felt like she didn't belong. She looked nothing like the other dancers. She wasn't dressed fancy like they were. And she wasn't nearly as confident either.

Ana was right. Chery didn't know anything about dance competitions.

Maybe Ana, or Day-Day, or anyone else with experience would have been a better representative for the school.

CHAPTER SIX

L IS FOR LAUGHINGSTOCK

Before long, Chery's name was called.
A tall man with pink hair waited by the
conference room door with a clipboard.

"Junior? Hip-hop?" he asked. "We need to
hurry. We're running behind." He confirmed
the name of the song and artist she would be
performing to.

Before Chery knew it, she was ushered
onstage. She was hit by bright lights, her
name was announced over the loudspeakers,
and someone offstage gave a ten-second
countdown.

Chery's stomach felt queasy, and she was still tired. She spotted the stern faces of the judges. Whenever she danced with her squad, people usually had smiles on their faces. Not frowns.

Then the beat hit. Automatically, Chery's leg lifted. She brought it down with a hard, deliberate stomp. She shuffled to the beat, just like she practiced. She jumped and flared her arms.

At the early break in the song, Chery froze with the music as choreographed. But, suddenly, everything left her brain. Including her moves!

What comes next? Chery's mind raced.

The audience's glare wasn't helping. Nor were the voices that suddenly popped into her head:

"Muscle memory," said Ana's voice.

"You'll be nervous," said Trina's.

"Forgot your moves," said Kai's voice.

"Keep the streak!" the school kids chanted in her mind.

The voices played in her head on an endless loop.

Chery's feet felt heavy. Her arms and shoulders felt weighed down. The beat came back. But she was still lost.

Then an image of the flash mob popped into her head. That crowd had loved them. Especially the guy who did the windmill. If she did a spin move like that, everyone might love her too.

I practiced it a few times, she thought. *Bet I can save this dance if I can pull it off!*

Chery got down on the floor. She spun her legs to start the backspin. But she didn't have enough energy to spin onto her shoulder. And she was too tired to lift her legs. She was like a turtle on its back trying to get up.

Chery looked for her mother's face in the crowd. If she saw her, she'd be okay. But Chery saw Kai instead. He looked between her and his phone and typed away.

Chery didn't want to be the laughingstock of the whole school. She quickly got up and ran off the stage. She hoped Kai hadn't seen her tears.

* * *

On the car ride home, Chery's ice cream melted in her lap. Her stomach was still in knots. Her mom had been wrong. Not even ice cream was enough to make her feel better.

"I used to rap," Mom said.

Chery looked sideways at her mom. But Mom's eyes were glued to the road.

"I had a partner named Sharon Moor," her mom said. "One day we decided to rap at our school's talent show. It was our freshman year of high school."

Mom paused as she merged into traffic. "Before that we only kicked rhymes in Sharon's basement. We did a lot of freestyle rapping. But onstage—during the talent show—we got tongue-tied."

Chery sat up. "Were you embarrassed?"

"Of course. And I never rapped again," Mom said. "But you know who didn't quit? MC Smile Moor."

Chery's eyes got wide. "The rapper and host of the *Rap Now* show? She was your rap partner?"

Mom nodded. "We were known as the Bea Moor Crew back then. The point is, I wish I hadn't let one bad experience derail my dreams. My old partner didn't. Like you, many people forget their dances. Others forget their speeches, or *raps*. The successful ones just don't give up. I wish I hadn't."

* * *

Back at home, Chery finally looked at the dance group text thread. Comments rolled in one after another:

What happened?

should have sent a real dancer

no more streak

is the school jinxed?

Chery felt horrible all over again. Mom just didn't understand. She had only let herself and her rap partner down. Chery had let down her entire team—and the whole school.

CHAPTER SEVEN

IN SYNC

At school on Monday, most kids were talking about Chery ending Ess Robinson Middle School's winning streak.

"We're jinxed," one of the cheerleaders said. "And the football game is on Friday."

Day-Day stopped by Chery's locker. "It'll blow over," he said.

But things didn't blow over. Kids whispered about it loud enough for Chery to hear. And at dance practice, Ana was staring at her every time Chery looked up.

Day-Day danced beside Chery.

"Why are you moving like that?" he whispered.

Chery raised her hand stiffly. She moved mechanically and counted every step.

"I'm dancing," she said, her voice lifeless. "Just like everyone else."

After class, Miss Miller pulled Chery aside. Like Chery's mother, Miss Miller told her a few stories about having stage fright. But it didn't comfort Chery. All the students were mad at her for ending the school's winning streak.

When Miss Miller finished her pep talk, Chery joined the team. They were discussing outfits for the regional team competition.

"Two words: solid gold," Ana said. "My aunt gets early access to the best stuff every season. She said we're bound to stand out. Also, if you place the order through DanceYes! you'll get half off."

Fran's dance catalog was passed around. Everything in it shimmered. Even the prices.

Chery had gone to a flea market for her last outfit. How could she get her mother to spend that kind of money? But after messing up at the competition, she didn't want to be the only negative voice.

Miss Miller locked eyes with Chery. Then she said, "Remember, hip-hop style is flexible and unique. The clothes you wear should reflect you. And everyone on the team should have a say."

"But my aunt knows what's hot in the dance world!" Ana said with a huff. "Anyone want to challenge her?"

The dancers looked at each other, but no one spoke.

Miss Miller looked directly at Chery as though she expected her to have something to add.

Chery shook her head. She had felt totally underdressed and out of place at the last dance competition. She was willing to listen to people like Ana and her aunt, who knew what to wear.

Chery would just have to convince Mom.

* * *

That night, Chery poured her favorite bean sauce over her rice. But she didn't eat it.

"What's wrong?" Mom asked.

"The dance team is wearing gold to the competition."

"Okay," Mom said, taking a bite of fried plantain. "There's this thrift store—"

"No!" Chery shouted. "It can't be from a thrift store or a flea market. It has to be from where everyone else buys it—DanceYes! And I know the reason I've never been in dance class before is because we can't afford it. But I can't stand out anymore."

Chery stopped talking when she felt her mom's warm hand rubbing her arm.

"If it's really that important to you, I'll do what I can to make it work," her mom said.

"Really?" Chery said.

"Really," Mom replied.

Things were finally working out. Her mother would make sure she was dressed like the team. And Chery would memorize the dance. Now she would be exactly like everyone else.

CHAPTER EIGHT

ALL GLITTER, NO GOLD

The next Friday, Chery and the rest of the team left school early and boarded a chartered bus. Because the team competition was in a neighboring state, they would be staying in a hotel.

When they arrived, they changed into their gold outfits for the dress rehearsal.

Many other teams wore gold outfits too.

Trina turned to Ana. "I thought we were ahead of the trend," she said.

"We're in trouble," Day-Day said.

"It gets worse," Kai said, holding a hand to one ear. "Hear that?"

The music blasting from several rooms down was familiar. They were songs the Ess Robinson dance team had chosen—a collection of the hottest songs on the radio. Other dance groups had chosen them too.

"How will we stand out now?" Fran asked.

"We just need to do something big," Ana said. "What if we put together a combination featuring all the latest dance moves?"

"Nope," Kai said. "Look online—those combination dances are everywhere."

Day-Day turned to Chery. "You always had a lot of ideas for our squad. What would you do?"

Everyone looked at Chery.

"Yeah, what would your squad do?" Trina asked.

"Last time I did it my way, I messed up," Chery said. "I don't think we should do it my way this time."

"We all get it wrong sometimes," Ana said. "Clearly, my aunt and I were wrong. But if you can think of a way for us to stand out and help us win, I'm in."

Chery thought about the flash mob dancers and why they stood out. They were unexpected. The dancers brought something memorable to their performance. And their song choices made people feel nostalgic.

Chery told the team about the flash mob. "And they wore street clothes," she added. "I think we should too. Hip-hop is street dance. And with our individual street style, we'll definitely stand out from all the teams wearing gold."

CHAPTER NINE

CHERY ON TOP

The next day, the hotel lobby shimmered with hundreds of kids dressed in their sparkling gold outfits. The Ess team dancers gathered in their assigned room. They looked like they were going to dance practice. They wore jeans, sweats, and leggings, paired with T-shirts, hoodies, and layered tank tops. And everyone wore sneakers.

"Are we sure we're doing this?" Ana asked. "My aunt said she'd be willing to give refunds if we don't wear the outfits to perform. But we still have them if we need them."

"Yeah, everyone's wearing gold but us," Fran said. "Maybe we should reconsider."

"My dad said we're making a bold choice and that he's proud of us," Nell said.

"And I saw a bunch of people pointing at us and nodding their heads," Kai said.

Chery took a deep breath. "When Day-Day and I had a squad, we always hustled. We did whatever it took to get our dances right. And we did well because—" she looked around at every team member, "we danced as a team."

"And teammates have each other's backs," Day-Day said. He stuck out his hand. Chery placed her hand on top of his. Ana put her hand on top of hers. One by one, the other team members followed.

"Go Ess team dancers!" everyone shouted.

After some last-minute practicing, Miss Miller brought the team to the room where the hip-hop competition was taking place.

While the Ess Dancers waited in the wings, they saw other performers onstage. The first hip-hop dance team competitors were amazing. All the popular moves were included in their routine. But the next three teams did the same thing.

When the Ess dancers took the stage, they started with a planned combination that Miss Miller helped them with. Everyone danced in sync. But then Kai and Liam turned toward each other.

"What are you doing?" Kai screamed.

"Dancing, you?" Liam yelled back.

Some people in the audience gasped.

Then the record scratched, and Day-Day shouted: "Dance-off!"

Old-school rap music played. Two by two, the dancers battled. Each pairing performed an improv they knew best. They infused their moves with hip-hop finesse and energy.

Kai's robot battled Day-Day's hip-hop ballroom moves. Trina and Nell battled tap dance moves by bouncing, stepping hard, and sliding. Jose's mix of samba and hip-hop dance moves battled Liam's blend of hip-hop and gymnastics.

Everyone was having so much fun, Chery didn't even realize that she and Ana were the last dancers left. Butterflies invaded Chery's stomach.

Ana walked toward Chery on her toes, just like when they battled in class. This time, Ana went hard with her shoulder pumps and hip thrusts. The audience clearly liked her fusion of hip-hop with ballet.

Ana brushed off her shoulders like she was dusting Chery off, but she smiled when she did it. She pulled Chery out to the front of the stage.

"Muscle memory," she silently mouthed.

The lights were still blinding, and Chery was still nervous. But she felt the beat thump in her heart. She couldn't help but move. Especially with Ana smiling at her while staring her down. The battle was on!

Chery's muscle memory clicked. Everything she'd practiced with her squad and team came back to her. She moved across the stage, dipping her knees, kicking out, and spinning.

At the bridge of the song, the music slowed. The team synced up and danced a practiced routine.

Then Chery grabbed Ana's hand and pulled her to the front of the group. They both looked at each other, and then they each lifted one of their legs and spun in opposite directions. Chery winked at Ana. Ana winked right back.

Both girls fell into splits, slid back up, and landed down with splits on opposite sides. Two perfect Cherys on Top!

The audience leaped to its feet with a round of thunderous applause.

Chery found her mother in the audience. Mom's smile was broad. And Chery's heart soared!

Thanks to her mom and Miss Miller, she hadn't quit the team. And thanks to her team's hip-hop hustle, they might have a shot at winning the competition.

AUTHOR BIO

photo by Vlad Andral

Dolores Andral was born in Brooklyn, New York, to Haitian parents. She loves reading, writing, and creating. Her hobbies include making clay dolls, teaching herself animation, and writing screenplays. Dolores earned an MFA from Queens University in Charlotte, North Carolina. After working on three adult novels, she never thought she'd write for children until she realized the need for her children to see themselves represented in books.

ILLUSTRATOR BIO

photo by Mario Gushiken

Mario Gushiken is a digital artist from São Paulo, Brazil. Drawing was a hobby for him as a child, and he is very happy to have turned it into his career. Inspired by cartoons and video games, Mario began working as a graphic designer and illustrator in 2014. In 2020, he became a full-time freelance illustrator. In his spare time, Mario likes to hang out with friends and play video games.

GLOSSARY

amateur (AM-uh-chur)—a person who is unskilled or only has a basic knowledge of an activity

ballerina (bal-uh-REE-nuh)—a female ballet dancer

ballet (ba-LAY)—a style of dance that tells a story through its movements

combination (kahm-buh-NAY-shun)—a group of dance moves that are linked together

fusion (FYOO-zhuhn)—the joining together of two elements

improvisation (im-prov-uh-ZAY-shuh)—making things up while performing

jinx (JINGKS)—to bring bad luck

nostalgic (noss-TAL-jik)—to think about the past and ponder how things have changed since then

showmanship (SHOH-min-ship)—the ability to entertain and perform

showstopper (SHOW-stop-uhr)—an act, song, or move during a performance that is exceptionally good

squad (SKWAHD)—a small group of people working together

DISCUSSION QUESTIONS

1. Chery is already a good dancer, and she had her own squad. Why do you think she was nervous about joining the school's dance team?

2. Chery was also nervous before her solo competition. What are some things she could have done besides texting and watching videos late at night to help her prepare?

3. Why did Chery's teammates warn her about the solo competition? Who do you think gave her the best advice and why?

WRITING PROMPTS

1. Day-Day suggested a dance battle to determine who would win a spot in the solo dance competition. But he didn't join in the competition. Write a paragraph about why you think he chose not to participate.

2. Chery lost her train of thought and forgot her moves during her first solo competition. Write about a time you lost confidence.

3. Chery was afraid to speak her mind and give her team another option once they discovered every team was wearing gold. Write a short paragraph about what might have happened if she had stayed quiet.

MORE ABOUT HIP-HOP DANCE

Hip-hop dance—sometimes known as street dance—is part of the wider umbrella of hip-hop culture. Hip-hop culture includes music, dress, speech, deejaying, emceeing, and dance.

Hip-hop can be traced back to the Bronx, New York, in the 1970s. Black, Caribbean, and Latino people would go to house parties where deejays played music. Dancing moved from houses to clubs and to the streets.

Breakdancing is a type of hip-hop dance that became popular in the 1980s. It became a worldwide sensation after two movies about the dance style were released.

Hip-hop dance borrows from many areas including African dance, jazz, modern dance, ballet, Salsa, Merengue, gymnastics, and more. Hip-hop dancers use the elements from many styles to make their dances their own.

Hip-hop doesn't rely on counting, rigid steps, or technical training. Dancers have an emotional connection to the music that guides their performance. And unlike many dance styles, hip-hop wasn't always taught in classes. But as it became more popular, studios started offering hip-hop dancing too.

Because hip-hop dancing is social in nature, it is also naturally competitive. Dancers teach and learn from each other. They push each other to become more creative. During dance battles, dancers may introduce their best moves, new moves, or new takes on moves.

Hip-hop fashion is also a fundamental part of hip-hop dance. Squads and dance crews often choose outfits to stand out from other squads during dance battles—which has led to fashion that is creative and constantly changing.